Spider Storch's
Music Mess

Gina Willner-Pardo
illustrated by Nick Sharratt

Albert Whitman & Company • Morton Grove, Illinois

Library of Congress Cataloging-in-Publication Data
Willner-Pardo, Gina.
Spider Storch's music mess / by Gina Willner-Pardo ;
illustrated by Nick Sharratt.
p. cm.
Summary: When his classmates make fun of him for playing the
flute, third-grader Spider Storch is determined to find a way to get
thrown out of his Music for Beginners class.
ISBN 0-8075-7583-6 (hardcover)
ISBN 0-8075-7584-4 (paperback)
[1. Schools--Fiction. 2. Behavior--Fiction.]
I. Sharratt, Nick, ill. II. Title.
PZ7.W6668Ss   1998
[Fic]—dc21 98-4994
CIP
AC

Designed by Scott Piehl.

To my kids, who give me goosebumps. —G. W.-P.

For Chris. —N. S.

Don't forget to read...

Spider Storch's
Teacher Torture

Spider Storch's
Carpool Catastrophe

Spider Storch's
Fumbled Field Trip

by Gina Willner-Pardo
illustrated by Nick Sharratt

Contents

1

1

Tubas Are Cool

"I bet if you stood right behind Mary Grace Brennerman and blew into a tuba as loud as you could, she'd jump three feet," I said.

"Then if she yelled at you, you could throw it at her," Zachary said. "Tubas are cool."

"I like the way they sound," Andrew said. "Like car horns."

Zachary puffed out his cheeks like he was blowing on something big. "The best thing to take in Music for Beginners is definitely tuba," he said.

We all agreed that when Miss Fry, the orchestra teacher, asked us what instrument we wanted to take, we'd say tuba.

After recess, we followed Ms. Schmidt to the auditorium. Music for Beginners was always in the

auditorium, across the courtyard from all the classrooms. This was because Music for Beginners was loud. Sometimes it didn't even sound like music. Sometimes it sounded like sick animals.

"Attention, class! Let's give Miss Fry our complete attention," Ms. Schmidt said. She pushed her hair off her forehead with the tips of her fingers. Ms. Schmidt has very long fingernails. Usually they are painted pink or red. Ms. Schmidt has to be careful about doing anything with her hands. Breaking a nail can ruin her whole week.

Miss Fry stood up. She had very short hair and long, dangly earrings. I bet Miss Fry couldn't wait for school to be over so she could take off those earrings and give her earlobes a rest.

"As you all know," Miss Fry said, "third-graders take Music for Beginners. Everyone is allowed to select an instrument. For the first few weeks, we will simply practice getting a good sound on our instruments. This is a lot more difficult than it looks."

I smiled inside. Music for Beginners was going to be a cinch. I could get anything to make a noise.

"Third grade is the perfect time to get your feet wet," Miss Fry said. "By the time fourth grade rolls around, you'll have a good feel for your instruments." She smiled and her earrings jiggled like mobiles.

"Ms. Schmidt will call your name, and you may tell her which instrument you would like to play," Miss Fry went on. Ms. Schmidt pointed to a poster hanging on the wall. "Please refer to this chart if you do not know the name of the instrument you want to learn," Ms. Schmidt said.

Regina Littlefield raised her hand.

"What's a bassoon?" she asked, squinting at the chart.

"A bassoon is a member of the woodwind family," Ms. Schmidt said. "It has a lovely tone."

"Oh," Regina said. "I thought it was one of those monkeys that pulls bugs off itself and eats them."

"That's a *baboon*, Regina," Ms. Schmidt said. "A bassoon is a long wooden tube. You blow into the mouthpiece. Two wooden reeds vibrate and create sound."

"Just so long as I'm not blowing on a monkey," Regina said.

Regina could be weird, but sometimes I agreed with her. You couldn't be too careful, especially in Music for Beginners.

Ms. Schmidt started to call out

names. Miranda Addison
play the oboe. Juan Alvare
to play the cello. Barbara Bo
wanted to play string bass. Mi
Fry wrote everything down on h
clipboard.

Mary Grace Brennerman
couldn't decide between the
violin and the viola. Actually, I think
she just wanted Miss Fry to know that
she knew they were two different instruments. Mary
Grace is always showing off
about how much she knows.
"I think I'll try the viola," Mary
Grace said. "Then when people ask
me why I'm playing the violin, I can
correct them."

That is just the kind of thing
Mary Grace loves to do.

ʟachary Finch," Ms. Schmidt called.

"Tuba!" Zachary yelled.

Miss Fry nodded as she wrote. Zachary looked at Andrew and me and smiled. I knew we were all thinking the same thing: how cool we would look playing tubas in the Junior Band Concert! Bands from different schools played for all the parents in the auditorium at night. Everybody clapped no matter how bad you sounded, and you got cookies and cider after.

Travis Hoffberg chose the drums. Regina Littlefield picked trombone.

"Andrew McMillan," Ms. Schmidt called.

"Tuba!" Andrew yelled.

"Sorry," Miss Fry said. "Zachary's

already picked the tuba."

"How come there can't be more than one tuba?" Andrew asked.

"Orchestras generally have only one tuba," Miss Fry said. "Besides, the school has just one tuba to loan out."

Uh-oh, I thought.

"You'll have to pick something else," Ms. Schmidt said.

Andrew scrunched up his face, thinking.

"Violin, I guess," he said.

I knew what he was thinking. At least with a violin, you could pretend you were hiding a gun in the case, like a gangster.

Violins were okay, but I was hoping for something louder.

"Joey Storch," Ms. Schmidt finally called.

I'd given up trying to get her to call me Spider.

"How about trumpet?" I said.

"We're out of trumpets," Miss Fry said.

 "French horn?"

"We're out of those, too."

"Being at the end of the alphabet stinks. There's nothing loud left," I said.

"How about viola? We have another viola," Miss Fry said.

"No, thanks," I said. No way was I sitting next to Mary Grace Brennerman for the rest of the year. "What else is there?"

Miss Fry looked at her list.

"Flute," she said, smiling.

"We always have plenty of flutes."

"Flute!" Flute was what girls played.

"Excellent, Joey," Miss Fry said. "I'll put you down for flute."

•

"Flute!" I said, biting into my salami sandwich. "Rats!"

"Why didn't you complain, Spider?" Zachary asked. "You're always complaining anyway. Why didn't you just ask for another instrument?"

"All the good ones were gone," I said. "Besides, I was afraid she'd make me take viola and sit next to Mary Grace Brennerman."

"Mary Grace would probably always be telling you what note you played wrong, and how to hold your bow," Andrew said. "You did the right thing."

"Yeah, but flute!"

"Maybe flute won't be so bad," Zachary said.

2

Playing the Flute

Flute was terrible. Flute was worse than when Mom made oxtail soup. Flute was worse than when Grandma Essie babysat and made me watch "Love Connection."

"Everyone calls me Twinkletoes," I said to Mom while she was fixing dinner. "That dumb old Miss Fry. I wish she'd *sit* on a flute."

Twinkletoes!

"Joseph Wolfgang Storch," Mom said, "you mind your manners."

Mom was taking me to the traveling arachnid exhibit at the zoo next weekend. This wasn't a good time to be a smart-mouth. Arachnid is another word for spider.

"Sorry," I said. Then, because I didn't want to look like I was giving in, I said, "I hate being called names."

"What was it the kids were calling you last month? Sugarlips?" Mom went back to shelling peas. "These things are over before you know it."

The kids called me Sugarlips because they thought I liked

22

Mary Grace Brennerman.
They finally stopped when
I passed around the
pictures I took of Mary
Grace picking her nose.

"I hate that stupid flute," I said.
"I can't get it to make any noise at all.
It sounds like air whooshing through
a hose."

"I'm sure all the flute players are
having a hard time," Mom said. "The
flute is difficult to play correctly."

"The girls play it fine. It's just me,"
I said.

"That's the most ridiculous thing
I've ever heard," Mom said. "Maybe if
you spent less time complaining and
more time practicing, you would be
able to get a good tone."

"I doubt it," I said. "If dumb old

Miss Fry had just let me play the tuba, none of this would be happening."

"Tubas are hard to play, too, Joey," Mom said.

"Not for boys," I said. "Tubas are *easy* for boys."

•

After a few weeks, my flute stopped whooshing. If I blew hard enough, I could get it to squeak. That was when Miss Fry started teaching us real songs, like "Mary Had a Little Lamb" and "Home on the Range."

"Home on the Range" was my favorite.

"I'd like to hear the flutes at the beginning," Miss Fry said.

Darcy Shapiro and Margaret Richardson sat up straight and

licked their lips. Margaret wiggled
her fingers. She'd been taking private
flute lessons since second grade.

Miss Fry held her baton high.

"One, two..." she counted.

We didn't get very far.

"Joey," Miss Fry said, "would you
try it again?"

"You mean by myself?"

"Please," Miss Fry said.

My face felt hot. I could see Mary
Grace giggling behind her viola.

I played the beginning of "Home on the Range" again. I blew hard. Maybe if I was loud, no one would notice about the squeaking.

"Thank you, Joey," Miss Fry said.

Darcy and Margaret were holding their hands over their ears. "That doesn't even sound like a flute," Darcy said. "It sounds like a police whistle."

Even Zachary and Andrew were laughing.

"That's enough, boys and girls," Miss Fry said sternly. She looked at me. "Maybe you can work a little more on your basics, Joey," she said.

"Are you sure there aren't any extra tubas lying around somewhere?" I asked.

From the look on

Miss Fry's face, I could tell that there wasn't even one tuba.

•

There was something I didn't tell Zachary or Andrew or even my mom. It was about the goosebumps.

Every time we played "Home on the Range," I got goosebumps. I could feel them on my arms. And little prickles on the back of my neck, like I was growing new hair.

GOOSEBUMPS!

I'd heard "Home on the Range" a million times. It never gave me goosebumps before.

It had something to do with playing it *myself*. Even if I did sound kind of squeaky or whooshy.

•

"Hey, Spider!" Zachary said at lunch. "Look what I found!" I uncrumpled the piece of paper. "Guess who this is?" it said. Then an arrow pointed to a picture of a boy with a spider on his shirt. He was wearing a skirt and a big floppy bow in his hair. And he was holding a flute.

"Hey! Who did this?" I asked.

"Beats me," Zachary said. "I found it under Mary Grace's desk."

"Those dumb old girls," I said.

"I think it's a picture of Twinkle-toes," Zachary said.

"This is going too far," I said. "I can't help playing the flute. Miss

Fry made me. I had no choice."

"You could have played viola," Andrew said.

"Like I would have wanted to sit next to Mary Grace for the rest of the year," I said.

"You know," Zachary said, "this really looks like you."

•

The only thing to do was this: make Miss Fry throw me out of Music for Beginners.

"How are you going to do that?" Andrew said. "Third-graders *have* to take Music for Beginners."

"I need to think about it," I said. "I'm pretty good at getting thrown out of things, though. Remember Cub Scouts? Remember Carpentry Club?"

"Yeah," Zachary said. "Mr. Lindner

said you shouldn't be left alone with a screwdriver until you're thirty."

I hunted around for the list of rules we had to follow in Music for Beginners. Usually I keep papers like that in balls at the bottom of my backpack in case I ever decide to read them.

"'All third-graders must arrive in the auditorium promptly. It is distracting to the other musicians when a student is late to class,'" I read. "See? I could be late all the time. Maybe that would work."

"It would drive Miss Fry crazy. That's for sure," Zachary said.

I smiled. If there was one thing I was great at, it was

driving grownups crazy.

I thought about the Junior Band Concert. If I got thrown out of Music for Beginners, I wouldn't get to go. I'd been looking forward to that concert. Mom and Dad were always dragging me to my sister Louise's gymnastics meets and soccer tournaments. It would've been fun seeing them clap for *me* for a change.

Then I thought about Mary Grace calling me Twinkletoes and drawing pictures of me in a dress. Something in my chest closed up.

"I have to get out," I said.

3

Twinkletoes Takes Action

Music for Beginners started at
11:00. I hid behind the dumpster on
the playground until 11:10.

When I got to the auditorium,
everyone was already halfway through
"Home on the Range." I stood at the
back of the room and listened for a
while. No goosebumps or anything.

I squeezed past Darcy Shapiro and
Margaret Richardson to get to my
seat. I tried to be quiet, but it was
hard. Music stands make a lot of noise
when you accidentally knock them
down.

Miss Fry stopped waving her
arms around. The music stopped.

"You're late, Joey," she said.
She put her hands on her hips
and gave me a dirty look.

"Sorry," I said. "I had to go to the bathroom."

A few people giggled.

"You have ten minutes at recess to go to the bathroom," Miss Fry said. "Please do not be late tomorrow."

The next day I got to the auditorium at 11:15.

"I thought I told you to go to the bathroom at recess," Miss Fry said.

"I did," I said. "I was getting a drink of water."

"For fifteen minutes?"

"Ouch!" Margaret yelled. "Joey, get off my foot!"

"Joseph Storch," Miss Fry said, "I'm running out of patience."

The next day I got to the auditorium at 11:20.

"That's it, Joey," Miss Fry said,

cracking her baton down
on her music stand.
"See me after class."

I couldn't help smiling
as I sank into my seat.
Getting thrown out of
Music for Beginners was
easier than I'd thought.

•

"I want you to practice your flute
an extra twenty minutes today," Miss
Fry said, "to make up for the twenty
minutes you missed this morning."

Up until now I hadn't been
practicing at all. It seemed kind of
stupid to tell Miss Fry that, though.

"I don't know if my mom will like
me having to practice more," I said.

"Oh?" Miss Fry said. "And why
is that?"

"I have an awful lot of chores," I said. "I have to mow the lawn and make my bed and do the  dishes and take out the garbage."

"My, my."

 "Sometimes I'm up until one o'clock in the morning, with everything I have to do," I said. "I don't know if I can squeeze in twenty extra minutes of practicing."

Miss Fry seemed to be thinking this over. "I guess you'll just have to practice at lunch recess," she said.

"Lunch recess!"

"Go right to the auditorium after you finish eating," Miss Fry said. "If you eat quickly, you can just about finish practicing before the bell."

•

"This stinks!" I said, finishing the last of my grapes. "Having to practice during recess!"

"You always say the wrong thing, Spider," Zachary said.

"You probably shouldn't have told her about having to stay up until one o'clock in the morning," Andrew said. "No kid has to do that."

"I was supposed to get thrown out of Music for Beginners," I said. "It's not fair."

"Punishments aren't supposed to be fair. They're supposed to be crummy," Zachary said. "They're supposed to make you stop doing whatever it is that the teacher doesn't like."

"I guess your plan bombed," Andrew said. "I guess you're stuck playing flute."

I stood up. I had exactly twenty-two minutes until the bell rang to finish practicing.

"Don't be too sure," I said. I smiled in an evil way, like a mad scientist. "We'll just see about that."

•

The auditorium was cool and quiet. You could barely hear the kids on the playground, laughing and yelling. They sounded far away, like they were in a whole other town, maybe.

The thick green curtains were pulled back from one window. Sunlight poured in and splotched the floor, and dust particles swirled like they were being stirred by an invisible spoon.

I'll bet there were trillions of dust
particles swirling in the sunny air.

I played "Home on the Range"
all the way through. Sometimes
it sounded squeaky. Sometimes it
sounded like I was blowing through
a straw. I didn't care. I liked hearing
music—*music I was making*—in a
quiet room. Most of the time I was
making too much noise to notice the
sounds of music and silence. Music—
even "Home on the Range" the way

I played it—was delicate and pretty.
Usually I wasn't too great with
delicate, pretty things. Usually
I broke them.

It was cool to be making something
delicate and pretty for a change.
I think that's where the goosebumps
were coming from.

I played "Home on the Range" until
the bell rang. My arms were covered
with goosebumps. You'd think all that
dust was snow—that I was sitting in
the middle of a blizzard—from all
those goosebumps.

•

 But I forgot about the sound and
the goosebumps the minute I came
back into class and saw Mary Grace
waving at me.

"Hi, Twinkletoes," she said.

I had my pride.

"If punishment is supposed to make you stop doing something, then I should spend all my time playing the flute," I said. "I should play it during Math and Spelling. I should carry it everywhere."

"Yeah!" Andrew said. "If Miss Fry thinks you're driving the whole class crazy, maybe she'll take it away!"

During Free Reading, when no one was looking, I pulled my flute out from under my desk. Very quietly I began to play.

"Joey," Ms. Schmidt said, "just what do you think you're doing?"

"Practicing," I said. "Miss Fry says I should practice more."

"I'm sure Miss Fry did not mean for you to practice during Free Reading."

"I can't help it," I said. "I love
practicing. I dream about practicing.
I love practicing more than anything.
More than spiders, even."

"It sounds like someone being eaten
alive by spiders," Regina Littlefield
said, "the way you play that thing."

"I appreciate your enthusiasm,
Joey," Ms. Schmidt said, "but you must
wait until 11:00 to play your flute. Or
I will have to speak with Miss Fry."

Between Free Reading and 11:00,
I got yelled at three times for playing

my flute. I could tell that Ms. Schmidt was really bugged. She started biting one of her nails.

After Music for Beginners, Miss Fry said, "Will you come see me, Joey?"

Some of the girls laughed.

"You're in trouble now, Twinkle-toes," Mary Grace said.

"I understand," Miss Fry said when everybody else had left the auditorium, "that you've been practicing diligently."

I had no idea what diligently meant, but I nodded anyway.

"According to Ms. Schmidt, a little *too* diligently," Miss Fry said.

"You said to practice more."

"I certainly did," Miss Fry said. "And I have some news for you."

"You do?" I tried not to look too

excited. I didn't want Miss Fry to think I *wanted* her to take away my flute.

"Ms. Schmidt and I have decided that you may be allowed to practice every day after lunch," Miss Fry said. She smiled like she had just given me a Christmas present.

"Every day?"

"In the auditorium, where you won't be disturbed," Miss Fry said. "Where you won't disturb anyone else."

"*Every day?*"

"You see?" Miss Fry said. Her smile stretched across her whole face like a great big rubber band. "Hard work really is rewarded."

I nodded miserably.

Miss Fry kept on talking about how

great it was to see a student trying
so hard, and how you didn't have to be
the best at something to enjoy doing it.

I barely listened. All I could think
was, Every day after lunch. *Every day*!

What was I doing wrong?

4

The Last Straw

I tried everything. On Tuesday
I pretended that my flute was a
submachine gun and that Mary Grace
Brennerman was a terrorist trying
to hijack a plane to Bolivia.

"Joey!" Ms. Schmidt said. "Put
your flute in the case where it
belongs!"

"And quit saying, 'Freeze, dirtbag!'"
Mary Grace said.

"A flute is not a toy," Ms. Schmidt said. "Don't make me remind you again."

•

"Children!" Miss Fry said, tapping her baton against her music stand. "What is that awful smell?"

"It smells like old food," Travis Hoffberg said.

"Old food that's been lying around in somebody's intestines for three weeks," Regina Littlefield said.

"Somebody who's dead," Travis added.

Margaret Richardson raised her hand.

"It's Joey. He took off his shoes," she said.

"And he isn't wearing any socks," Darcy Shapiro said. "It smells like

rotten meat back here."

"I can't play unless I'm comfortable," I said.

"Joey," Miss Fry said, "please put on your shoes. This isn't the beach."

"How can I play if my feet are all hot and sweaty?" I asked.

"You'll just have to find a way," Miss Fry said.

•

"Joseph Storch!" Ms. Schmidt yelled. "Take your flute out of your nose!"

"But I was only pretending—"

"I don't want to hear it." Ms. Schmidt closed her eyes, like my mom does when she has a headache. "You're going to have to learn to treat your flute more carefully."

"Joey's always sticking things up his nose. Not just his flute. Once he tried to stuff three straws up one nostril," Mary Grace said.

"Shut up, Mary Grace," I said. "Nobody cares what you have to say!"

"I don't like that kind of talk, Joey," Ms. Schmidt said. "And I don't like your attitude. If you want to stay in Music for Beginners, you're going to have to start behaving yourself."

Mary Grace stuck her tongue out at me, but I didn't even tell on her.

Ms. Schmidt had said *If you want to stay*. I was getting close.

•

Thursday was the last straw.

"That's it, Joey," Ms. Schmidt said. "Let's have it."

"You mean my flute?"

"Yes." Ms. Schmidt held out her hand.

"I wasn't really going to hit any baseballs with it," I explained. "I was just pretending."

"No more excuses, Joey. I'm through talking." Ms. Schmidt sighed. "You're obviously just not mature enough to take care of a musical instrument."

I knew what mature meant: grown-up.

"I am *so* mature enough," I said.

I placed the flute gently in Ms. Schmidt's outstretched hand. I felt a little sad. It surprised me.

Ms. Schmidt laid my flute on her desk.

"I'm pretty disappointed in you, Joey," she said. "Miss Fry was really beginning to hear some progress."

"*I* still think you sounded like a sick cow," Regina said.

"That's enough, Regina." Ms. Schmidt turned to me. "Tomorrow, when the rest of the class goes to the auditorium at 11:00, you will come back here," she said. "You can spend the time reading."

"All alone?"

"*I'll* be here," Ms. Schmidt said. She was smiling an evil smile. She looked exactly like a mad scientist.

5

Traveling Arachnids

"Congratulations," Zachary said.

"I knew you could do it," Andrew said. "If there's one kid who can get himself thrown out of something, it's you, Spider."

"Thanks," I said. "I don't like the idea of sitting in the classroom all alone with Ms. Schmidt, though."

"Yeah. Her eyes just staring at you,

no matter where you sit," Zachary
said. He shivered.

"I saw a movie like that once,"
Andrew said. "This doll was mad
because she couldn't be a real little
girl. So she pretended to be a grown-
up lady and stared at all the girls in
the toy store until she drilled holes in
their heads."

"Cool," Zachary said.

"Smoke came out of the girls' heads.
They got all melty, like big old
candles," Andrew said.

"I bet Ms. Schmidt could
stare at you like that,"
Zachary said, "until your
eyeballs dripped off your
face like big globs of wax."

"Bet she couldn't," I said. But
I wasn't as sure as I sounded.

On Friday, when morning recess was over, I watched as all the third-graders headed across the courtyard to the auditorium. I hid behind a bush as they all walked past me. I didn't want them to see me. To think I was scared of heading back to the class-room alone. I wasn't scared. That wasn't it at all.

I watched as they all trooped into the auditorium. Then it was quiet for a while. The sun was shining through the tops of the trees. It was almost like being in a park. It made me think of all the people—ladies with babies, old people—who didn't have to go to school on a sparkly, sunny day. Who could sit under a tree whenever they wanted and not feel like they were

breaking any rules.

Finally I heard it. I listened carefully. "Home on the Range" didn't sound any better without me. It didn't sound any worse, but it didn't sound any better, either.

For some reason, I was glad. I looked down at my arms. Not a goosebump in sight.

•

"How was it?" Zachary asked at lunch.

"How was what?"

"You know. Being alone. With *her*."
Zachary made his eyes bulge out of his
head. "The crazy doll-lady."

"Not so bad." I took a bite of a
peanut-butter cracker and brushed
the crumbs off my lips. "She yelled at
me for being late back to class. Then
she made me read something about
seeds."

"Boring. We learned the beginning
of 'You're a Grand Old Flag,'" Andrew
said.

I love that song.

"Miss Fry passed out invitations to
the Junior Band Concert," Zachary
said. "We have to wear *ties*."

"I don't even have a tie," Andrew
said.

I did. A red bow tie.
I wore it every Christmas.

Mom said it made me look handsome.

I loved looking handsome. I'd never told anyone that. No one would have believed it. Most people don't think I'm the kind of kid who cares how he looks.

It was totally unfair that Zachary and Andrew got to look handsome *and* get cookies and cider all on the same night.

•

The next day was Saturday. Saturday was the day Mom was taking me to the traveling arachnid exhibit.

At the breakfast table Mom said to Dad, "Are you sure you wouldn't like to join us?"

Dad poured more cereal. "I've got to put the finishing touches on the

Hansen bid this afternoon," he said. "I just don't think I can get away."

"Aw, come on," I said.

Dad sighed. "You know I'd love to go, Joey. You *know* I'd love to have the chance to look at spiders that aren't crawling out of my own shower drain. But I just can't today."

He really did seem disappointed.

"You wouldn't catch me in the same room with those stupid spiders," Louise said. "Who wants to look at a bunch of hairy old spiders anyway?

Besides, Heidi Michaelson and I are doing something way cooler than looking at some dopey bugs."

"*Arachnids*. How many times do I have to tell you? Not bugs. *Arachnids*." I wiped milk off my lip with my arm. "What are you doing that's so cool?"

This would be good. Louise never did anything cool.

"We're going to make a band. Heidi and Dory Deluise and Emily Killian and I are all going to be in it."

"How can *you* make a band? You don't know how to play anything," I said. I thought, Wait'll I tell Zachary and Andrew.

"We're going to call ourselves The Heartbreakers," Louise said. "Heidi plays drums. Dory plays clarinet. Emily plays piano. *I* sing."

"You? Sing?" I laughed so hard
I started to choke. "You can't sing."

"I can, too!"

"Not in tune!" I screamed. "Not so it
sounds like singing!"

Louise looked
really mad. "Heidi
says I have a great
voice," she said.
"Heidi says I sound like
Madonna probably sounded
when *she* was in the fifth grade!"

"Maybe Heidi is going deaf! Maybe
Heidi should have her hearing
checked!" My stomach hurt
from laughing so hard.
"You? Madonna?"

"Mom!" Louise said.
"Make Joey stop!"

"You can't sing!

You stink at singing," I said.

"Joseph Wolfgang Storch," Mom said. "That's enough."

I almost said, "You should call yourselves The *Window*breakers!" It was right on the tip of my tongue. But I stopped myself. And not because of Mom calling me by all three names, either.

I just didn't feel like saying it anymore.

•

The exhibit was great. I saw tarantulas and scorpions and trap-doors and purse webs and jumpers and spitters. I saw crab spiders and bolas spiders. I saw a net-casting spider that looked just like part of the plant it was lying on. I saw a female black widow guarding her egg sac.

In nature, after they hatch, the stronger baby spiders eat the weaker ones.

"If Louise and I were spiders, I'd have already eaten her for lunch," I said.

Mom sighed. "Joey—"

"No, I wouldn't," I said. I was in too good a mood to want to make Mom mad. "I'd have spit her out, probably."

"Well, that's nice to hear."

"I'd probably be dying for a cheese sandwich anyway," I said.

Mom squeezed my shoulders close as we walked toward the next cage.

"Having fun?" she asked.

I smiled up at her. "All these spiders!" Thirty-two cages of them. I'd already counted. "It's like Christmas and my birthday and the last day of school all mushed together."

Mom laughed. Then she pointed at my arm. "Look," she said.

"What?"

"Goosebumps."

I looked. I hadn't even noticed. "All these spiders," I said again.

Mom nodded. Her arm was still around my shoulders, hugging me.

"You're lucky," she said.

"I am?"

"Loving something that much. Knowing what it is that makes you happy. Not many people know."

"They don't?"

Mom looked at me and smiled. "You're lucky that you know what makes you happy," she said. "Some people live a lifetime and never know."

"That's sad," I said. I felt funny inside. It was hard to talk about feelings.

"Very sad." Mom squinted at the writing over the next cage. "Isn't this a funnel web spider?"

It was. Funnel webs are my favorites. I watched the one in the cage as it began to eat a frog.

I felt very, very lucky.

6

Lucky

At 11:00 on Monday I stood at Ms. Schmidt's desk. I waited until she looked up from checking vocabulary worksheets.

"Yes, Joey?"

"I was wondering," I said, "what I could do to get back into Music for Beginners."

Ms. Schmidt put her pen down and tapped the tips of her fingers together. Her fingernails made little clicking noises against each other.

"I don't know, Joey," she said. "You were asked to leave the orchestra because you weren't behaving like a responsible third-grader."

"I know. But I've changed. I'm more responsible now."

"Really?"

"Really." I tried to think of how to convince Ms. Schmidt. "I've matured."

"In one weekend?"

"*Please*." There was no way to prove anything. "I'm different. I know..." I paused. "*Now* I know what I like."

"Joey," Ms. Schmidt said. "If—and I have to speak with Miss Fry—*if* we let you attend Music for Beginners, how will things be different?

"Well," I said, thinking hard, "I'll practice fifteen minutes after school. Every day. And I won't ever pretend my flute is a baseball bat or a gun."

"That's a start."

"And I'll keep it in the case. Always. I'll only take it out to play it and clean spit out of it."

"That sounds reasonable."

"Plus I'll never take my shoes off during rehearsals or be late or not pay attention or—"

Ms. Schmidt held up her hand.

"As I said, I have to speak with Miss Fry," she said. "But I think I can safely say that we'd both like to give you another chance."

"What're you going to do about Mary Grace calling you Twinkletoes?" Andrew asked on the way to school the next day.

"Maybe take more pictures of her picking her nose. Maybe start a rumor that she has webbed feet." I shrugged. "I'll think of something."

"You always do," Zachary said.

Andrew and I waited while Zachary lowered the front end of his wagon and slid his tuba case over it. Then he tipped the wagon back up, and we

made our way down the sidewalk toward the school.

"I wish I played the flute," he said. "I'm sick of hauling this tuba everywhere."

"My knees are black and blue from my violin case banging against them every morning," Andrew said. "A flute case is smaller than a lunchbox."

I smiled. I still wished I played the tuba. I couldn't help it. I liked the way the notes shook and rumbled in your bones. I liked that it was big, that people always pointed and said "Hey, look at the tuba!" when someone played one in a parade.

But the flute was okay. I wasn't sure that playing the tuba would give me goosebumps.

Andrew looked at my flute case sticking out of the top of my backpack.

"Maybe you're really lucky after all," he said.

"I know," I said, smiling.

7

Junior Band Concert

At the Junior Band Concert, "Home on the Range" sounded great. I only squeaked once. Maybe twice.

The audience clapped and clapped. I could see Mom and Dad and Louise in the second row. Mom wore her sparkly dress. Dad was smiling and shouting "Bravo!"

They found us after the concert.

"You boys were wonderful!" Dad said, smiling proudly. "I've never heard 'Home on the Range' sound better."

"That was 'Home on the Range?'" Louise said.

"And don't you all look handsome!" Mom said.

Zachary and Andrew and I smiled. We felt a little goofy in our ties and shirts with buttons. But it was fun being the center of attention when we  hadn't done anything wrong.

"Let's get cookies," I said, when it seemed like Mom was finished staring and smiling at us.

"Try not to spill," Mom called after me.

At the snack table, Zachary and Andrew and I were seeing how many peanut-butter crisps we could stuff into our mouths at one time when Mary Grace and Regina came over. They were wearing dresses made out of the same material as my Grandma Essie's couch and shiny shoes.

"You guys look different," I said, rolling up my sleeves and spitting peanut-butter crumbs.

"Gross, Joey," Mary Grace said, brushing crumbs off her front. Then she looked up and smiled. "Isn't it amazing how Regina and I both have velvet dresses, only hers is green and mine is blue?"

Zachary and Andrew and I nodded and looked at the floor. Mary Grace was always asking questions that had no answers.

"I hate wearing dresses," Regina said. "My knees get cold."

I thought about telling Regina she looked dumb in a dress.

"Green velvet looks like moss," I said instead.

I thought she'd say something about how she'd deck me if I tried to touch it, but she didn't.

"You sounded okay, Joey," she said.

"Thanks." I was surprised. Girls didn't usually say nice things.

"Not like someone being eaten alive by spiders," she said.

"More like a cat being run over by a car," Mary Grace said.

"Not like a cat," Regina said. "You sounded like someone playing a real flute."

A real flute. I liked that.

"Hey," Mary Grace said, pointing at my arm. "How come you're all bumpy? It's hot in here."

"I don't know," I said. I shoved my sleeves down. Then, to get her to stop looking at me, I said, "Do you know that in the whole world, you're never more than three feet away from a spider?"

"That's a lie, Joey Storch, and I'm telling!" Mary Grace said. Her face got all red. She turned around and stomped into the crowd.

"Great, Spider," Andrew said.
"What'd you have to say that for?"

"You know Spider," Regina said.
"He's always saying dumb stuff."

I thought about arguing with her.
I thought about telling her there was
something hanging out of her nose.

But I didn't. I just smiled.

Goosebumps'll make you do that.

black widow

bolas spider

crab spider

funnel web spider

jumping spider

net-casting spider

purse web spider

spitting spider

scorpion

tarantula

trapdoor spider